D0401909

Learning to Read, Step by Step!

 Ready to Read Preschool–Kindergarten
• big type and easy words • rhyme and rhythm • picture clues
For children who know the alphabet and are eager to
begin reading.

 Reading with Help Preschool–Grade 1
• basic vocabulary • short sentences • simple stories
For children who recognize familiar words and sound out
new words with help.

 Reading on Your Own Grades 1–3
• engaging characters • easy-to-follow plots • popular topics
For children who are ready to read on their own.

 Reading Paragraphs Grades 2–3
• challenging vocabulary • short paragraphs • exciting stories
For newly independent readers who read simple sentences
with confidence.

 Ready for Chapters Grades 2–4
• chapters • longer paragraphs • full-color art
For children who want to take the plunge into chapter books
but still like colorful pictures.

STEP INTO READING® is designed to give every child a successful
reading experience. The grade levels are only guides. Children can progress
through the steps at their own speed, developing confidence in their
reading, no matter what their grade.

Remember, a lifetime love of reading starts with a single step!

For Christopher and Annie

Copyright © 2002 by Martha Weston.
All rights reserved under International and Pan-American Copyright Conventions.
Published in the United States by Random House Children's Books, a division of
Random House, Inc., New York, and simultaneously in Canada by Random House
of Canada Limited, Toronto.

www.stepintoreading.com

Educators and librarians, for a variety of teaching tools, visit us at
www.randomhouse.com/teachers

Library of Congress Cataloging-in-Publication Data
Weston, Martha.
Jack and Jill and Big Dog Bill : a phonics reader / by Martha Weston.   p.   cm. —
(Step into reading. A step 1 book)
SUMMARY: Jack and Jill enjoy sledding until their dog gets tired.
ISBN 0-375-81248-2 (trade) — ISBN 0-375-91248-7 (lib. bdg.)
[1. Dogs—Fiction.   2. Sleds—Fiction.]
I. Title.   II. Step into reading. Step 1 book.
PZ7.W52645   Jae   2003   [E]—dc21   2002013223

Printed in the United States of America   15 14

STEP INTO READING, RANDOM HOUSE, and the Random House colophon are registered
trademarks of Random House, Inc.

STEP INTO READING®

STEP 1

Jack and Jill and Big Dog Bill

A Phonics Reader

by Martha Weston

Random House New York

Jack and Jill
and Big Dog Bill
go up, up, up the hill.

"Pull, Bill!" says Jill.

At the top,
they stop.

"Go, Bill!" say
Jack and Jill.
So Jack and Jill
and Big Dog Bill
go down, down, down
the hill.

BUMP.

PLOP.

They all stop.

"More, more!" says Jack.

Jack and Jill
and Big Dog Bill
go up, up, up the hill.

"Push, Bill!" says Jill.

At the top,
they stop.

"Go, Bill!" says Jill.

Jack and Jill
and Big Dog Bill
go down, down, down
the hill.

BUMP.

PLOP.

They all stop.

"More!" says Jack.

"More!" says Jill.

"Oh, no," say Jack
and Jill.
"Bill will not go!"

Jack and Jill
and Big Dog Bill
go up, up, up the hill.

"Push, Jack!" says Jill.

"Pull, Jill!" says Jack.

At the top,
they stop.

Jack and Jill
and Big Dog Bill
go down, down, down
the hill.

BUMP.

PLOP.

They all stop.

"No more hill!"

say Jack and Jill.

Jack and Jill
and Big Dog Bill
go home.